CAN ROAD TRIP

MN
WI
MI
IA
HOME!
IL
IN
OH
MO
KY
WV
VA
SMOKY MOUNTAINS
NC
TN
AR
SC
MISSISSIPPI RIVER
AL
GA
MS
LA

ME
VT
NH
NY
MA
RI
CT
NJ
DE
MD

PA

FL

① EVERGLADES NAT'L PARK

National Park

PARKS to VISIT
① Everglades/FL
② Big Bend/TX
③ Grand Canyon/AZ
④ Yellowstone/WY
⑤ Yosemite/CA

To my dear friends—Regan, Peggy, Jane Ann, and Marge—
with happy memories of our hikes in the national parks
—L.W.B.

M.L.H. & P.L.H.—For allowing me to see our big,
beautiful world through your beautiful, bright eyes

B.B.—For being my wild life partner and making even
a Dallas sewer drain a fun place to play

G.W.B.—For camp-outs in the front yard in Maine
and night walks at the lake

H.C.H.—For proposing to me when the sun first rose in Acadia

And Mom—For passing your love
of all things beautiful on to me
—J.B.H.

To my beloved brother, Martin,
who took me on my first cross-country adventure

And a warm thanks to my models,
Meg, Jeff, Ben, Graysen, and Amy
—J.R.

Our Great Big Backyard
Text copyright © 2016 by Laura Bush and Jenna Bush Hager
Illustrations copyright © 2016 by Jacqueline Rogers
All rights reserved. Manufactured in China.
No part of this book may be used or reproduced in any manner whatsoever
without written permission except in the case of brief quotations embodied in
critical articles and reviews. For information address HarperCollins Children's
Books, a division of HarperCollins Publishers, 195 Broadway, New York, NY 10007.
www.harpercollinschildrens.com
Library of Congress Control Number: 2015959760
ISBN 978-0-06-246835-2 (trade bdg.)
ISBN 978-0-06-246836-9 (lib. bdg.)
ISBN 978-0-06-246841-3 (pbk.)
The artist used pen, ink, watercolor, gouache, and marker
to create the illustrations for this book.
Typography by Amy Ryan
16 SCP 2
❖
First Edition

LAURA BUSH AND JENNA BUSH HAGER

Our Great Big
BACKYARD

Illustrated by
Jacqueline Rogers

HARPER

An Imprint of HarperCollinsPublishers

"**H**uddle!" my BFF, Hank, said. "I have our whole glorious summer mapped out."

Hank's Summer Plans

Hank wanted to watch a different movie every day.

Ricky was going to create a YouTube channel.

Louise and I couldn't wait to have an epic Starship tournament.

It was going to be the best summer of our lives.

But that was before. . . .

That night, Mom gave me the bad news. "We are going to spend the summer on a road trip!"

Dad's map was different from Hank's.

"But I was supposed to spend it with my friends!"

"Jane, there is more to life than staring at a screen. You'll love being on the open road."

As if I didn't have enough to worry about, my pest of a brother, Sam, kept bothering me.

"Come on, Jane, let's go outside! We'll practice camping."

"No way. I'm busy."

On the last day of school, my parents picked me up for what they called **"The Great American Road Trip."**

BEAR
XING
11.25

I'm leaving on a road trip.
Don't know when I'll be back again.
Oh boy, I hate to go.

I sent my friends a message:

As we drove south, my parents sang along to show tunes. How humiliating! At least I had their phone to keep me company.

"Jane, put that away. You're missing some beautiful sights."

"All I am missing is time with my friends!"

FIRST STOP:
Everglades National Park.
Swamps, cypress trees with creepy hanging moss, and mosquitoes as far as the eye could see. Big deal.

There's absolutely nothing to see here!

We drove **FOREVER** to get to our next stop. As we crossed the Mississippi River, Sam waved to a riverboat captain.

I hid behind my iPad.

NEXT STOP: Big Bend National Park.

I couldn't wait to get out of the car so I could finally play Starship.

"Jane, please put that away. Come look through the telescope!"

The stars
at night are
big and bright

The sky in Texas was huge and **bright**. Then, bless
my lucky stars, a meteor shower lit up the sky like
fireworks—brighter than any screen I had ever seen.

We traveled west across the desert. Sam and I
pretended we were astronauts on Mars.

NEXT STOP: Grand Canyon National Park.

We tiptoed over the Skywalk like acrobats on a tightrope.* The river so far below looked like a shiny ribbon.

As we explored I sent a selfie to my crew.

Yep, that's me on Blaze, my mule. The only thing missing is you. XOXO

When we rafted down the Colorado River, I was a pirate captain with Sam as my first mate, navigating treacherous waters.

NEXT STOP: Yellowstone National Park.

We were park rangers on the lookout for animals.

*Americans call this a buffalo, but it is a bison.

We waited and we waited for Old Faithful to explode into the air.
Then **finally** . . .

5, 4, 3, 2, 1 . . .

BLAST OFF!

It was like a real Starship shooting off into space!

LAST STOP: Yosemite National Park.
Sam and I served our last dinner on the road.
Fireflies hung in the air like fluttering stars. We
pretended we were cowboys.

The mountain went up and up and up, straight into the sky, watching over us. I felt really small but really great, too, like I was part of something big.

OH NOOO!!!

The next morning I couldn't find my most prized possession, my tablet.

"Jane, you packed it away a week ago," Mom said.

"What did you like best?" I asked Sam.
"The campfires!"
I thought about all the stars.
"I'm going to miss our big adventure."

I was sad when we got home. But then I took Baxter into our backyard, and I had a brilliant idea.

"Mom, can my friends come over for a camp-out?"

I told Hank and Ricky and Louise
ALL about the places we'd seen.
**"I had the best summer after all!
It's spectacular out there."**

Just then, a shooting star **ZOOMED** across the sky.
"Look! It's beautiful right here in our own backyard."

Alabama
Russell Cave National Monument

Alaska
Denali National Park
Gates of the Arctic National Park
Glacier Bay National Park • Katmai National Park
Kenai Fjords National Park • Kobuk Valley National Park
Lake Clark National Park • Wrangell—St. Elias National Park
Sitka National Historical Park

American Samoa
National Park of American Samoa

Arizona
Grand Canyon National Park
Petrified Forest National Park • Saguaro National Park
Tumacacori National Historical Park

Arkansas
Hot Springs National Park

California
Channel Islands National Park
Joshua Tree National Park • Lassen Volcanic National Park
Pinnacles National Park • Redwood National Park
Sequoia National Park • Kings Canyon National Park
Yosemite National Park
Rosie the Riveter/World War II Home Front
National Historical Park
San Francisco Maritime National Historical Park

Colorado
Black Canyon of the Gunnison National Park
Great Sand Dunes National Park
Mesa Verde National Park • Rocky Mountain National Park

Connecticut
Weir Farm National Historic Site

Delaware
First State National Historical Park

District of Columbia
Chesapeake and Ohio Canal National Historical Park
(with Maryland and West Virginia)

Florida
Biscayne National Park • Dry Tortugas National Park
Everglades National Park

Georgia
Ocmulgee National Monument

Guam
War in the Pacific National Historical Park

Hawaii
Haleakalā National Park • Hawai'i Volcanoes National Park
Kalaupapa National Historical Park
Kaloko-Honokohau National Historical Park
Pu'ukoholā Heiau National Historic Site

Idaho
Nez Perce National Historical Park

Illinois
Lincoln Home National Historic Site

Indiana
George Rogers Clark National Historical Park

Iowa
Effigy Mounds National Monument

Kansas
Tallgrass Prairie National Preserve

Kentucky
Mammoth Cave National Park
Abraham Lincoln Birthplace National Historic Site

Louisiana
Cane River Creole National Historical Park
Jean Lafitte National Historical Park
New Orleans Jazz National Historical Park

Maine
Acadia National Park

Maryland
Harriet Tubman Underground Railroad
National Monument

Massachusetts
Adams National Historical Park
Boston National Historical Park
Lowell National Historical Park
Minute Man National Historical Park
New Bedford Whaling National Historical Park

Michigan
Isle Royale National Park
Keweenaw National Historical Park

Minnesota
Voyageurs National Park

Mississippi
Natchez National Historical Park

Missouri
Jefferson National Expansion Memorial

Montana
Glacier National Park

R OWN BACKYARD. **GET OUT THERE!**

Nebraska
Homestead National Monument of America

Nevada
Death Valley National Park (with California)
Great Basin National Park

New Hampshire
Saint-Gaudens National Historic Site

New Jersey
Edison National Historical Park
Morristown National Historical Park
Paterson Great Falls National Historical Park

New Mexico
Carlsbad Caverns National Park
Chaco Culture National Historical Park
Pecos National Historical Park

New York
Saratoga National Historical Park
Women's Rights National Historical Park

North Carolina
Great Smoky Mountains National Park
(with Tennessee)

North Dakota
Theodore Roosevelt National Park

Ohio
Cuyahoga Valley National Park
Dayton Aviation Heritage National Historical Park
Hopewell Culture National Historical Park

Oklahoma
Washita Battlefield National Historic Site

Oregon
Crater Lake National Park
Lewis and Clark National Historical Park (with Washington)

Pennsylvania
Independence National Historical Park
Valley Forge National Historical Park

Rhode Island
Blackstone River Valley National Heritage Corridor

South Carolina
Congaree National Park

South Dakota
Badlands National Park
Wind Cave National Park

Tennessee
Cumberland Gap National Historical Park
(with Kentucky and Virginia)
Manhattan Project National Historical Park
(with New Mexico and Washington)

Texas
Big Bend National Park • Guadalupe Mountains National Park
Lyndon B. Johnson National Historical Park
Palo Alto Battlefield National Historical Park
San Antonio Missions National Historical Park

Utah
Arches National Park • Bryce Canyon National Park
Canyonlands National Park • Capitol Reef National Park
Zion National Park

Vermont
Marsh-Billings-Rockefeller National Historical Park

Virginia
Shenandoah National Park
Appomattox Court House National Historical Park
Cedar Creek and Belle Grove National Historical Park
Colonial National Historical Park

Virgin Islands
Virgin Islands National Park
Salt River Bay National Historical Park

Washington
Mount Rainier National Park
North Cascades National Park • Olympic National Park
Klondike Gold Rush National Historical Park (with Alaska)
San Juan Island National Historical Park

West Virginia
Harpers Ferry National Historical Park (with Maryland and Virginia)

Wisconsin
Apostle Islands National Lakeshore

Wyoming
Grand Teton National Park
Yellowstone National Park (with Montana and Idaho)

THERE'S MORE!
No matter where you live in the United States,
there is a National Park Service site for you.

**Find your park at
www.findyourpark.com.**

**The National Park Service wants
Every Kid in a Park. Plan a field trip with
www.everykidinapark.gov.**

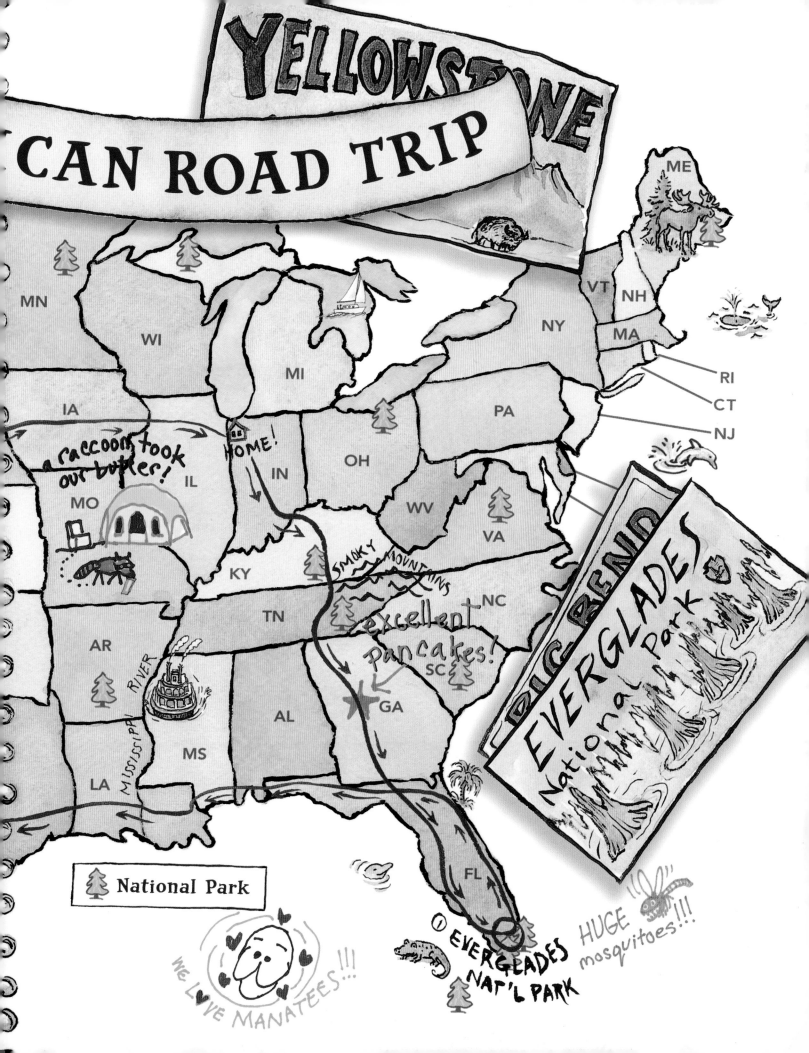